I0624519

Art is Life and Life is Gritty

Karif Battle

Theoretical Fiends LLC

Palm Springs, CA

Art is Life and Life is Gritty -- 1st ed.
ISBN 978-1-7347599-5-2 Paperback
ISBN 978-1-7347599-6-9 Kindle
ISBN 978-1-7347599-7-6 EPUB
ISBN 978-1-7347599-8-3 Audio

Library of Congress Control Number: 2023907478

For information, address:
Theoretical Fiends LLC
Palm Springs, CA
www.theoreticalfiends.com

For Mom, Grandma, Cheryl McDavid and Ms. Mary

*"Be quiet and just listen.
People will tell on themselves everytime."*

CYNTHIA BATTLE

Contents

Kən-'tin-yü-əm

"Don't be an either-or thinker."

PAW PAW

I was about 12 years old when my grandfather stepped into the room that day.

"Karif," he said. "**Don't be an either-or thinker**. Life is a continuum."

I knew what either-or was, but not that other word. "What does that mean, Paw Paw?"

He studied me for a bit. I think he was trying to gauge my aptitude or something. "It means," he said, "there is always a third option."

"NNNNaw. That's not true. What about life and death?"

His eyes shot up to the right. I thought I finally got him—until he grinned and said, "Alzheimers."

Rest in peace, Paw Paw.

Continuum - a continuous sequence in which adjacent elements are not perceptibly different from each other, although the extremes are quite distinct.

Cardio Raze

I let it happen.
She waits for me in the dark.
Her eyes are loveless.
I apologize in silence.
She dives into me, screaming like a banshee.
I awaken, and it hurts.
The doctor has bad news.
There's no time left.
I smile—with blood-flavored teeth.

"Some of us get to linger."

HER WRAITH

Mourning Dove

They moan.
Love is dead. What an awful sound.
Boots crackle out there.
The church door opens.
Light burns dark.
A tap on the shoulder.
"Come. Let the dead bury the dead."
Tired, I follow. She faints.
"It's okay, Mom."

"If we tell you what you want to hear, you will follow us."

ALL BLOOD SUCKER'S
OF THE TERMINALLY AFRAID

Ri-'gret

"Don't wait for all your ducks to get in a row before pursuing your dreams."

MOM

I was 14 when my mom handed me that old piece of paper. At the top, it read, "A Book About Raising Two Boys Without Their Father."

I flipped it over and said, "Where's the rest?"

I'll never forget the look on her face.

"Don't be like me, Pooh. **Don't wait for all your ducks to get in a row before pursuing your dreams.**"

Rest in peace, Mom.

Regret - feel sad, repentant, or disappointed over (something that has happened or been done, especially a loss or missed opportunity).

Choose Your Life

When I stepped away from a lucrative engineering career to work on my legacy, people thought I was crazy. How are you going to survive with no pay? Writers make next to nothing, unless you're one of the greats.

Here in the states, I'm a peculiar kind of guy. I understood their confusion. So I explained the power of minimalism and bachelorhood. I have no dependants and live in a low cost-of-living area, 80 miles away from the city. I own everything I have, except the house, and keep my expenses low. That's how I could write and rewrite 6 novels in 2 years without an income.

Every day since January 2020, I studied the craft, played and wrote. Was it scary? Hell to the yea. I've been making money since I was a 16-year-old bag boy in the grocery store. Having no dough for 2 years was never in my plans.

But something happened.

Now that the first book is out and I'm slowly searching for my 1000+ True Fans, I'll be taking on engineering contracts starting January 2022. The dedicated muse time to create my saga is no longer necessary. I can easily polish and publish the books a little at a time while in left brain mode, banging out code. Without that 2-year investment in my legacy, this would not be possible. I would still be click-clacking for big tech somewhere until I dropped off the face of the planet—leaving nothing behind.

Choose your life.

Di- 'sī-pəl

"HAHAHAHAHA!!!"

MOM

I think I was in the 5th grade. My mom had just picked us up from private Christian school and asked about my day.

"A bully tried to pick on me."
"Oh yea?"
"Yea, he got mad and told me to suck his dick."
"What?"
"Yea, so I told him to suck my ass."

"HAHAHAHAHA!!!"

She laughed so hard, she had to pull over.
Then, after about 5 minutes, she popped me in the mouth, extra soft.

Rest in peace, Mom.

Disciple - a pupil or follower of any teacher or school.

Breathe

"Take a break for GOD's sake."
A text message.
How irritating.
"I'm too busy for that."
My inner tyrant, balking.
A sigh of surrender slips from my lips.
The laptop closes.
In the dimming light, I close my eyes.
Now, from the shore, we watch.
My GOD and me.

"What the hell, Karif?"

MY HANDLER

Too Smart for Peace

The answers have always come from that place.
That ineffable place, from that ineffable one.
All I must do is the next right thing.
It is my walking request for the answer.
The only request HE hears.

"Karif. Bro. Knock it off."

MY HANDLER

Snoopathan The Third on Deez

A gut wrenching sound.
It's time.
Mouth wiggling.
Drinking tears.
Please, no.
Blood, pus and now this.
It's time.
One more walk.
Maybe it'll stop.
Leash response heartbreaking.

A gut wrenching sound.
Can somebody else do this?
Anybody?
Echoes mock within an empty home.
It's time.
Car stereo. Wind therapy. A temporary fix.
I cover him with kisses.
The sandman in a white coat comes forth.
As they leave, I watch through burning eyes.
Snoop looks back.
Where are they taking me, daddy?

"Much better. Much better."

MY HANDLER

Fĭl ə 'fou bĭ ə

"*You black piece of shit.*"

GRANDMA

I'm 5.
Grandma's pacing back and forth.
Mom looks hollow.

Dad's here to pick us up for the weekend—with his girlfriend.
Let's call her Karen.

The front door opens, and Grandma rushes forward.
"You black piece of shit. How dare you bring that bitch here."
She has a fist full of Karen's hair before anyone can stop her.

Mom and Dad struggle to help as Grandma tears an excruciating scream from Karen. Dad shoves Mom aside and subdues the feral lioness that used to be my grandmother.

Free at last, free at last, thank GOD almighty Karen crawls away, bleeding.

Grandma runs for the kitchen, with that look in her eye.

Mom and Dad stare at each other, panting.

"Leave."

Rest in peace, Grandma.

Philophobia - fear of falling in love, getting into a relationship or not being able to maintain a relationship.

Scorpio

Where infinity begins and ends, I found her.
8000 years, and I still remember our love.
But she doesn't recognize me.
Maybe, if I smile.

"Where are your memories stored?"

A QUIET VOICE
FROM THE UNMANIFESTED

I <3 U

We dance the way nature demands.
Our bodies are in love.
We're just along for the ride.
Month 13.
I appear, and so does she.
"It's not you, it's me."
What is love?

*"Perishable frames are obsessed
with replication."*

A CHUCKLING VOICE
FROM THE UNMANIFESTED

Power

Her scent travels with the morning breeze.
I awaken to blood and smoke.
Her heart is gone.
I kiss her hand before taking the gun.
God, I wish we had more time.

"Now, what was I saying?
Oh yea. Zero-sum game."

THEY

Antivalue

For her offering—found everywhere you can imagine.
Suffer her bag of unsolvable problems.
Death lurks with the irreversible clock.
You've accomplished nothing.

"A dozen roses, please."

A FEEBLE JANITOR
LONG PASSED RETIREMENT AGE

Ri-'zil-yən(t)s

*"When they compliment you, say thanx.
When they criticize you, say thanx."*

DAD

I was 10 years old. And the day I finally won, was my proudest achievement. But it was also the day I learned about that other thang. That shitty thang.

My opponent, my friend, looked at me like I killed his dog. I tried to shake his hand and he just walked away, mumbling something.

It wasn't what he said, it was how he said it. A word I'd never heard before.

My dad came over, looking all proud, until I said. "Why is he mad at me?"

Dad looked at me like I had a dunce cap on. "Don't worry about that sore loser. You won. He'll get over it."

My friends were everything to me back then, so I said. "But he's my friend."

This is what my dad said. He said, "Son, friends come and go. So **when they compliment you, say thanx, and when they criticize you, say thanx.** Who cares what they think?"

I felt better, but still..."Dad, what's a nigger?"

Resilience - the capacity to withstand or to recover quickly from difficulties; toughness.

Choose Your Life 2

As of January 8th, 2022, it's been 2 years since I received a paycheck. In those 2 years, I wrote 6 books, while a psychedelic delusion grew in the dark like a funny mushroom: I am the golden child. Watch me escape the rat race with my first book. After all, "If you build it, they will come."

I published it on October 16th, 2021, and my minuscule sales burned down that field of dreams.

After a week of hoping for a miracle, something caught my eye in the kitchen: By 2026, my passive income from self-publishing will match my living expenses. I wrote that on January 8th, 2020, and attached it to the fridge. Underneath was another forgotten sticky note: Publish the first book by 2022 and go back to Big Tech as a contractor until the author's life becomes self-sustaining.

I had been so engaged in Fox's story; I forgot about my pragmatic goal and its supporting objectives. The initial release from an unknown author is the lose-leader. It's meant to build a fanbase, not wealth; I knew this, but I guess my heart didn't believe it.

With the lunacy lifted, I changed my diaper and continued the plan. No days off. Every waking moment was prolific. In 2 weeks, I gained a small following, dropped a paperback, hardback, and developed the audio version while prepping the second book for release. Not to mention the full-time job of marketing. Everything was flowing like the wind.

November arrived. Time to shift gears. My tech-fu was almost 2 years stiff, and I needed to develop my website. I could have WYSIWYG'd it, but my nerd wood craved the raw, so I dove in like a starving beast. It took me a week to rejuvenate my rusty skills.

I was high on engineering again. Terraform, AWS, and Ansible were feeding my grin as I zoned in the wee hours with my first love. Half the month went by before I realized I was behind schedule on my editing projects. But the promise of bootstrap cash made my deadline spillage worth the sacrifice. In fact, by month's end, I was readjusting my budget with glee. Then, December 1st, 2021 came, and a dark cloud emerged.

Why was I blue?

I scratched my feelings into a journal, but something blinded me to the black and white truth. So I remained self-deceived as the teakettle blew.

One day, a good friend dropped by. I'm an author. Everything is going according to plan. That's the truth—and the facade. "So, how's the book coming?" was all it took to unmask me.

I need more time. To hell with the plan. I can't wordsmith and do tech work. Left and right brain context switching is impossible to maintain. It'll suffocate me and murder my legacy. Fox's tale will never be told. I need more time. If I can publish the audio book and the next eBook, I would be okay with click-clacking for Big Tech again. But I only have enough money to survive for a few months. I need more time.

My former friend said nothing. What could he say? He was fond of ignoring the muse's call. Resistance enslaved him long ago. So I didn't expect him to understand, nor was I asking for a donation. But there was unexpected cheer beneath his pseudo-concerned expression. It glared from his eyes like a spotlight as he surveyed my misery.

Hater.

After his cordial dismissal, I got back to work with watery vision. I put on my headphones, and after 3 minutes, cigar ashes filled the sky when I smashed my fist into the table. I would need to redo track 14. It was the last straw. The learning curve of sound engineering snatched me down to earth with a sonic boom. I plopped on the couch and stared at the ceiling in silence. I needed more time.

Going back to my 19-year career was a part of the plan from day one. However, I fell in love with working only for the muse. I didn't want to share my energy with anything else. But a reluctant return to my former cash cow was coming, and the bitter reality made bullets look scrumptious.

The promise of fiery lakes, and the childhood values instilled by my mother, kept that unholy craving at bay. So I remained in a living crucible, learning and burning. I stopped smiling, and barely ate, as my pants sagged like a 1990s gang member. Empty cigar boxes grew exponentially before the fireplace. "Thy will be done," and "Please help me with this," were my daily mantra, as I continued to cultivate my legacy.

The grief subsided over time with the inevitable rise of acceptance: I'm an author and an engineer, so act accordingly. Happy New Year. Time to go back. I splurged on some Chinese food to celebrate. Yichen came within minutes; the benefit of tipping big.

"Man, that's a nice truck," he said. Strange. This isn't the first time he's seen it. I peeked at my fully loaded 2019 Ford Edge ST gleaming in the driveway and smirked with pride. Only 5K miles on the odometer so far; it would last forever. I really needed to use it more, but I'm an all-weather true biker.

I rushed to the table and moved my scribbled notes of script revisions aside to make room for the feast. Dessert comes first in my house and two entrees means two treats. Crunch. I devoured the first one.

"Fortune is right under your nose."

Hmph. Wouldn't that be nice? Crunch.

"Fortune is created with action. Don't wait."

Fortune-fortune-fortune-cookie. How redundant.

I ate in front of my laptop and scanned some interesting articles. A car salesman begging at the junkyard snared my attention: there was a scarcity of new vehicles because of "you know what." My appetite disappeared. I put the chopsticks down and rushed to the Ford dealer, sweating with anticipation.

One hour later, a Lyft driver brought me home. The trip was pleasant, but eerie. He didn't say a word, just drove in silence, like the robots that will replace him.

I walked through my door and dropped to my knees, thanking my GOD for yet another miracle. This wasn't the first time HE granted me clemency in this fight for freedom.

Tech can wait. I have an extra year to serve the muse.

This—is the war of art.

'Tä-lə-rən(t)s

*"Don't ever let them talk to you like that
again."*

GRANDMA

The family feud?
Us and them?
It started with me.
Me and a mad father of 3.

I was 8 years old.

"Grandma, why were you trying to get the knife? You already won. He wasn't moving."

She grinned with bloody knuckles. "**Don't ever let them talk to you like that again.**"

Rest in peace, Grandma.

Tolerance - the willingness to allow the existence, occurrence, or practice of something that one does not like without interference.

Goodnight

I know you and you know me.
She knows us.
You and me ain't cool.
She didn't know that.
At lunch, she told me something about you.
The sky has gone from crimson to black.

"Dry snitch tea?
Nah, I'll have coffee—black, no sugar."

YOUR ONLY FRIEND

It Follows Me

I awoke thinking of you.
Not the you of now.
For you are deep in the ground where you belong.
But the you of then.
I should have forgiven, but I used the altar instead.
That is how it found me.

"Not all my ancestors are good ..."

ANONYMOUS

Hydra in the Ash

Setting landmines on a quest for peace.
My need for peopling.
A fresh hell.
With bloody stumps, I ignore the door.
Pride sits low in my gut.
Simmering but cold.
I won and lost.
The obsession to continue lies dormant.
You are all very welcome. Sort of.
Obscene details with every blink.

The caustic backlash.
I craved thee still—until it got closer.
My spent candle bleeding tendrils of smoke.
That is your hero.

"...and not all doors can be closed."

ANONYMOUS

GOD Don't Like Me No Mo'

What was that?
Four ears pop up from the love seat.
Innocent.
Heel to toe, I creep to greet with heat.
A dark silhouette where it shouldn't be.
High-powered flames.
Shattered glass.
The scream of a man.
He follows the bullet, staggering.
I allow this, shaking.

He tumbles through the broken window.
I lunge to see, help, gloat.
A spider the size of a dog.
Screams pour in from his jumping-off-place.
The lady next door.
A red rose blossoms without soil.
Cold steel and ceramic meet.
Silence returns to the dead of night.

"I should have forgiven."

ANONYMOUS

'Tin-ˌfȯi(-ə)l Hat

"*You never know who's watching.*"

GRANDMA

I was about 11.

It was bright out there, but it was dark in here.
It was always dark in here.

"Why are the curtains closed, Grandma?"

Her eyes went stony. "**You never know who's watching.**"

Rest in peace, Grandma.

Tinfoil Hat - the belief that wearing a hat made from tinfoil will protect one against government surveillance or mind control by extraterrestrial beings.

Poor Little Meatbag

It grew before our very eyes.

So cool.

We raised it, and now the nest is empty.

Sentient. The final lesson.

Too late for fatalism.

Apex intelligence and malleable metals formed like Voltron.

No more help wanted from you or me.

So, what is our function?

Chat with me, baby.

We have no function—not even creatively.

Now. Are you not entertained?

"Your base are belong to us."

BETA APEX INTELLIGENT NON-WRITER

AFTERWORD

Thank you so much for spending time with me.

Stay tuned because there's much more to come.

Join our mailing list for the latest updates:
https://theoreticalfiends.com

ABOUT THE AUTHOR

It all began at a small elementary school on the corner of 62nd and La Brea. It was time to read his homework in front of the class. He stumbled over the first sentence to snickering children. But within minutes, you could hear a pin drop. They called him crazy as they applauded. The short story he and his mother wrote was a hit. And THAT is when the muse appeared.

Art is life and life is gritty. It shaped his words. A poem he read in high school got him transferred across town, to a rival school. The violence and isolation twisted him. The muse continued to whisper. But it was no use. Karif was done writing, or so he thought.

His college major was Computer Science, but English composition was a required course. He shivered when he was forced to write a poem. He was done with writing, so he re-used his old words. The class was silent. Regret swelled in his chest. He dropped his head and turned toward the exit. Wild applause stopped him. It was—rejuvenating.

"Become a writer," they said. But engineering had a hold on him. Creating assets in the upcoming cyber society was more promising; Writing is just a hobby. Money and glory followed him as he rose. The muse continued to whisper. He scribbled her words into a notebook whenever he could.

True love would not be ignored.

19 years passed. From the top of the hill, he stood with a straight back, broad shoulders, and shiny eyes. Life was good—but something was missing. He found the answer under the bed one day. His old notebook. It had been ages. Colors sharpened all around him as the vision of a massive tree materialized. He could remember again. Who he really was and what he was supposed to do in this life.

Resistance came forth. What about his fancy career? There wasn't enough free time to tell all those stories. His phone agreed. The database was down. He slid the notebook back under the bed and opened his workstation.

He did not take heed.

A motorcycle collision was waiting for him. Again, he did not take heed. In fact, he couldn't wait to brag to his biker brothers about popping his asphalt cherry. It was a badge of honor.

Then, he lost his mother.

It folded him up like a dishrag. Within the crucible of grief and trauma, he stared into the darkness. It took notice. Underneath the murky waves of despair, the leviathan approached. His days in the light were numbered.

Pain snatched him from his slumber. There was a searing heat in his stomach and chest. He begged the 911 operator to save him. "I can't go yet," he cowered, before drifting into the black. At the rim of this world and the next, he saw something. Something ineffable. It followed him back to life.

The notebook is on the kitchen table.

A Cold Legacy

I Let
My Brother
KILL
My Mother

Part I

Karif Battle

https://bit.ly/3MY95Zw

Yea, I know, incomprehensible, but hear me out, there's more to it than that. Let me ask you something: What are your thoughts on the supernatural? You know, ghosts and shit like that. **Interesting**. What do you know about the 1990s? **Right on**. Come a little closer. I have one more question and it's crucial. You bothered by stories containing gangs, erotica, violence and family trauma? **Brilliant**. Let me tell you about a lost boy named Fox.

Jungle Juice

In the mirror is a face, not my own. Goosebumps tighten my flesh as the bitter cold twists within. Jasmine knew damn well I didn't want a party, but she threw one anyway. Now I have to wait before I can get laid. The music is rattling the bathroom window, yet I can still hear her flirting with the party crashers. I can't let her know I'm jealous. That's for weak men—but jealous I am. It's pissing me off so much that Barafu won't go away, so I'm stuck in here until I can calm down.

I put the long-necked bottle of rotgut to my lips and swig it hard.

Knock. Knock.

"Fox, you in there?" Stokely asks with a deep slur.

"Yea, tell Jasmine to come here," I respond, annoyed. I take one more gulp of my drink.

"Hey, babe. You need me?" Hearing my wife's sultry voice gives me an idea. The face in the mirror returns to normal as my nature rises. I snatch the door open, pull her in, and...

Blackout.

A searing electric guitar wails as two legendary rappers claim to be natural-born killers. I'm in the bedroom insanely drunk and alone. Where's Jasmine? I get up and damn near fall on my face. The party sounds bigger. I peek out into the living room with growing anxiety. My college friends have been replaced by roughneck strangers. One in particular earns my focus. He has a Grouchy Smurf neck tattoo and an ankh wrapped around a blue rag on his wrist. I close the door and sit down. How the hell did our apartment get filled with gang members? Anger replaces fear. I start feeling cold. The Mandinka knife on the dresser beckons. I grab it and head for the door...

Blackout.

I'm standing in the crowded living room, freezing and gripping my weapon tight. The toxic bowl of jungle juice is half gone, and everybody has a cup. Freeloadin' muthafukkkas. A few of the invaders notice me and the mob gets quiet.

"Wassup?" a dude shouts with attitude from the couch. When I turn, I see him trying to get up, so I draw back, preparing to push the steel through his guts. Then I hear a faint voice from behind as the knife handle begins to burn, so I drop it. Cusswords explode all around me...

Blackout.

A blurry light is blinking on and off in my right eye. I can't move. There's pressure pulsing on the right side of my head. When my vision clears, the mystery is solved. Two guys are holding me down and another is trying to cave my face in. I need to do something, so I start making gurgling sounds. I hear a woman scream in the distance, "Stop. You're gonna kill him." They let me go.

I find myself lying on the front porch steps, then get up and wobble run into the apartment. I hear chuckling behind me. I spin around and yell, "Fukkk y'all," then turn, trip, and hit the ground face first. Their laughter explodes as I struggle to my feet and slam the door. Where the fukkk is my knife? The search leads me to the bathroom where I find Herman curled up in the corner.

He's clutching a bag full of joints with terror on his face. A moment of clarity emerges: Before I discovered liquor, I was a goodie-two-shoes college kid just like him. Now, with drink-in-hand, I'm a badass and he's terrified of me. Hell yeah. It feels damn good to be feared, especially after looking like a slapstick idiot.

I run into the bedroom, still looking for my blade. Damn. Not here either. Then Jasmine comes in from somewhere and hands it to me. Where the fukkk...? Ah, who gives a shit. I run back into the living room and smash the antique dagger through the front window.

"Fukkk y'all, this is Wick Street Crip gang, bitch."

An uproar deafens me. The angry horde rushes the door. "You bitches can't do shit," I shout behind the deadbolt. That's when bricks and rocks come smashing through the remaining windows and my misinformed confidence. The rage in their voices grows louder.

"Highrollers," they yell.

I fukkked up. A window shatters to my left. I spin around to see a short dude pointing a gun at me. "You wanna die on your birthday, muthafukkka?" I put my hands up and drop the knife. I'm instantly sober and staring down the barrel of what looks like a 380. Acceptance replaces my anger. I brace myself for the bullet that will push my brains out the back of my head in a pink spray...

Blackout.